My Naughty Little Puppy

Playtime for Rascal

Gulp!

For Tom ~ H.W.
For Fi and Morris ~ K.P.

WooF
magazine

ISBN 978-0-545-49079-5

12 11 10 9 8 7 6 5 4 3 2 1   12 13 14 15 16 17/0

40

Printed in the U.S.A.
First Scholastic printing, November 2012

My Naughty Little Puppy

Playtime for Rascal

Holly Webb

Illustrated by
Kate Pankhurst

SCHOLASTIC INC.

Chapter One

Frisbee Fun

"Come on, Ellie! Chase it!" Max shouted. "Just jump up and grab the Frisbee!"

Ellie did her best, racing across the grass, but Max had thrown the bright yellow Frisbee as hard as he could, and it was curving around. She looked behind her anxiously, trying to see where it would land.

"Wrong way!" Lila yelled, starting to dash after the Frisbee, too. "Ellie, you can get it if you run!"

My Naughty Little Puppy

Ellie could hear Max behind her, muttering about how bad she was at Frisbee, and her cheeks turned pink. Why did her older brother and sister have to be so athletic? Max took it all so seriously, too, when it was just supposed to be fun!

Then she started to giggle. Rascal, her Jack Russell puppy, was galloping after the Frisbee, too.

He launched himself into the air and grabbed the Frisbee in his jaws while he was a foot and a half off the ground. He landed on all four paws, looking very pleased with himself.

"Wow, Ellie, your dog's a lot better at catching than you are," Max teased. "Here, Rascal, give it to me, boy."

My Naughty Little Puppy

Rascal looked up at Max, the Frisbee hanging out of his mouth. It was almost as big as he was, and his shiny black eyes sparkled over the top of it. He shook his head wildly, swinging the Frisbee back and forth.

"I think he might be trying to kill your Frisbee, Max." Lila giggled.

Max bent down and grasped the Frisbee—but Rascal came with it, hanging on by his teeth.

"Put him down, Max! You'll hurt his mouth!" Ellie cried. "Rascal, come on, let's play some more. Give it to me!"

Back on the ground, Rascal eyed Ellie thoughtfully and spat the Frisbee into her hand. Then he stood there wagging his tail

My Naughty Little Puppy

hopefully and staring up at them.

Max grinned. "Okay, Rascal, this one's for you, boy!" He flicked his wrist, sending the Frisbee curving out over the grass. Rascal hurled himself after it. He managed to grab it just as it was about to hit the ground, and then scampered back, dragging it along behind him in his teeth.

"He's so good!" Lila said, and Ellie glowed with pride. Her older brother and sister loved Rascal, but they spent a lot of time moaning about how naughty he was. Rascal was a monster when it came to chewing things, especially shoes.

My Naughty Little Puppy

"That was awesome," Max said as Rascal trotted off, the Frisbee still in his mouth. "We just need to explain to Rascal that he's supposed to give the Frisbee back!"

Ellie told her best friend, Christy, all about the Frisbee session at school on Monday. "Have you ever tried playing Frisbee with Bouncer?" she asked. Bouncer was Christy's beautiful Labrador.

Christy looked thoughtful. "He's amazing at fetching, but he only really likes chasing sticks."

"It was really funny." Ellie laughed. "Rascal flipped himself right over in the air

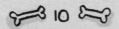

to get one catch." She put her chin on her hands. "It stopped Max and Lila from complaining about how bad I was at catching it, anyway. I wish I was better at sports!"

Christy shook her head. "You can't be good at everything, Ellie! You're an artistic person."

Mrs. Harley finished taking attendance. "Now for some exciting news, everybody. Mr. Turner's just been telling all the staff about Field Day!"

Ellie stared at Mrs. Harley in horror. Field Day! She'd almost forgotten that it was that time of year. "Oh, no . . ." she murmured.

Christy put her hand over her mouth, trying not to laugh. "Sorry!" she whispered.

My Naughty Little Puppy

"But it is funny that you were *just* telling me how much you hate playing sports!"

"So over this week and next week, we'll be practicing a lot for Field Day," Mrs. Harley went on. "And this year, with the Olympics coming up soon, we've got a special project, too!"

Ellie looked up at their teacher anxiously. Not more sports!

My Naughty Little Puppy

"I'd like you all to create something really special related to the Olympics. It could be a piece of writing, a painting, some music—whatever you like."

Christy stuck her hand in the air. "Mrs. Harley, can we work together?"

Mrs. Harley nodded. "No more than three in a group, though, please. And your project needs to be handed in next Thursday, the day before Field Day. Then Mr. Turner will pick the best project in each grade, and they'll be on display at Field Day."

Ellie looked at her friend hopefully. At least Christy was athletic! If they did their project together, it might not be so bad. It was just a shame they couldn't team up for Field Day!

Chapter Two

Ellie's Athletic Plan

Mom brought Rascal with her when she came to pick up Ellie. Max was staying late for soccer and getting a ride later, and Christy was coming home with them to hang out.

"We can start on the project!" Christy said excitedly.

Ellie made a face.

"What's the matter?" Mom asked. "What kind of project is it?"

"One about sports." Ellie sighed. "Field

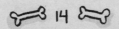

My Naughty Little Puppy

Day is at the end of next week. We have a note to parents asking if you want to come and watch. You don't, do you?"

"Of course I do!" Mom gave her a sympathetic smile. "Are you really not looking forward to it?"

Ellie shuddered. "You can watch Max. I don't want anyone watching me come in last place in everything."

"You won't!" Mom laughed.

Ellie gave her a look. She had been last in everything the year before—it had been awful.

"But you don't have to be athletic for the project," Christy said. "It's just about the Olympics. Maybe we could do a comic about it. I'll write and you can draw."

Ellie nodded. "That could be fun."

My Naughty Little Puppy

"Or we could make a sculpture or model."

"Oooh, yes!" exclaimed Ellie.

Rascal looked up, his tail wagging wildly. The girls' voices were making him feel jumpy and excited, and he suddenly shot off down the road, pulling Ellie along with him.

My Naughty Little Puppy

Ellie raced behind him, panting, "Rascal, stop!" But he didn't, not until they reached the corner, where there was a good lamppost to sniff. Then he looked up at her, his dark eyes glinting naughtily.

"You can run really fast when you've got Rascal pulling you!" said Christy as she caught up with Ellie. "Maybe you should ask Mrs. Harley if we can have a race with our dogs on Field Day."

Ellie looked down at Rascal thoughtfully. She couldn't see Mrs. Harley agreeing to that, but maybe Rascal could help her practice. He was definitely better at running and catching things than she was!

"So what should we make?" Ellie asked, putting her drawing things out on her desk. She looked down at Christy, who was sitting on the floor, tickling Rascal.

"You tell me!" said Christy. "I know it's a sports project, but you're the one who's good at making things."

"We could make the Olympic stadium in London," Ellie suggested. "I've got some sheets of card stock that were in this great craft kit that Aunt Jenna gave me."

"That's a great idea," said Christy, jumping to her feet. "Let's ask your mom if we can look up the stadium online."

A few minutes later, Christy and Ellie were staring at the computer screen in Ellie's mom's little office under the stairs.

Christy wrinkled her nose. "You're sure that if we make a model of that it won't just look like a huge doughnut?" she asked.

Ellie shook her head. "Not if we paint it all silver."

"Your dinner's ready, girls!" Mom called from the kitchen.

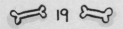

My Naughty Little Puppy

Max had just gotten home from soccer
and was sitting at the table looking hungry
as the girls came in with Rascal behind them.

"Heard about Field Day?" he asked
Ellie, smirking. He loved Field Day, and
usually won at least two races.

Ellie turned pink. "Yes," she muttered.
The look on Max's face made her even
more determined to practice with Rascal.
She was going to try to win something
this year! Or at least not come in last . . .

Lila wandered in, reading a magazine.
"Hello, Christy. Oh, you have Field Day
soon, Ellie? They should do things like
dancing, too. It's totally unfair to people
who don't like running."

Ellie nodded. She definitely agreed.

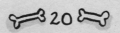

My Naughty Little Puppy

"Hey!" Christy squeaked, making Ellie jump. "Where did my sausage go?"

Ellie leaned down to look under the table. Rascal looked back at her and gave a huge gulp, the last of Christy's sausage disappearing quickly between his white teeth. He eyed her guiltily.

"Sorry, Christy! Here, you can have mine. How did he even get up there without us noticing?" Ellie asked.

Lila shrugged. "He must have jumped onto Dad's chair, and just stuck his nose up and grabbed it. He's a monster. Do you want some of my beans, Ellie, if Christy's having your sausage?"

My Naughty Little Puppy

"Yes, please." Ellie peered back under the table. "Rascal, you're a piglet!" Then she smiled to herself. He needed to keep his strength up for running!

Back in her room, while they were finishing a plan for their model Olympic stadium, Ellie told Christy her idea to practice for Field Day with Rascal.

"That's a great idea!" cried Christy. "Can Bouncer and I join in, too? We could all go to the park on Saturday."

"That would be fun," Ellie replied. But secretly she planned to practice in her yard before Saturday, too, to make sure she didn't embarrass herself.

Chapter Three

The Big Dog Race

"What's Ellie doing out there with Rascal?" Granddad asked, staring out of the kitchen window into the yard.

Mom came over to look. "Oh! She's preparing for Field Day. She's been practicing with Rascal all week."

Out in the yard, Ellie and Rascal raced up to the lilac tree and back. As Ellie reached the patio, she looked up and spotted Granddad. She waved and trailed

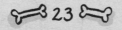

over to the kitchen door, Rascal trotting behind her. Even *he* looked tired.

"Working hard for Field Day, huh?" Granddad asked as he gave her a hug.

Ellie nodded. "I just want to get a little faster. And we've been practicing boot-throwing, too—that's one of the events."

"Don't you get to practice at school?" Granddad asked.

My Naughty Little Puppy

"Oh, yes!" Ellie blushed. "But at school
I get really nervous because everyone's
watching, and that makes me even worse."

Granddad nodded. "I'm sure practicing
will help. But it's not the end of the world
if you don't win, you know. I was never a
very fast runner. I got better at it as I grew,
though—maybe you will, too, Ellie."

Ellie sighed. Maybe she would, but
she wasn't going to get any taller by next
Friday. . . .

"Anyway, I've got a present—look! A
new leash for Rascal. It's an extendable
one, so you can go running in the park with
him."

Ellie beamed and gave him a hug.
"Thanks, Granddad! I'm going to the park with
Christy tomorrow—we can try it out then."

 25

My Naughty Little Puppy

"Rascal, stop pulling or I'll drop everything!"
Ellie was trying to hold Rascal and carry all
the stuff she'd brought for their Field Day
practice at the park. Of course, Rascal had
chosen that moment to forget about walking
to heel. It didn't help that he was on his
special new leash. It was very cool—the
plastic handle had a leash inside that pulled
out to twenty-six feet long! Ellie was finding it
a little tricky, though, because if she pressed
the button by mistake, it extended when she
didn't mean it to.

"Here, I'll take the water bottles."
Christy grabbed them just before they
slipped out of Ellie's arms.

"Thanks! Oh, I'm glad
we're here," Ellie said as they
entered the park. She put down the rest
of her things and gazed around. Lots of
people were doing sports. A couple of girls
were Rollerblading, and there was a man
in bright yellow sneakers jogging along the
path.

Rascal growled quietly, and Ellie
looked down at him. "What's up, Rascal?"

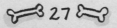

My Naughty Little Puppy

"I think it's that jogger," Christy
whispered. "I don't think Rascal likes his
shoes!"

Ellie crouched down to pet Rascal
and tell him it was okay, but Rascal wasn't
paying attention. His lips were lifting back
from his teeth as he growled, making him
look really fierce. As the jogger ran past
them on the path, Rascal suddenly barked

My Naughty Little Puppy

loudly and shot after him. Ellie dropped
the plastic handle of his leash, and then
grabbed it again with a sigh of relief—but
the button must have banged on the path,
and the leash started to extend.

"Oh, no!" Ellie gasped as Rascal set off
after the jogger and his sneakers, barking
wildly. "Rascal, come back," she called
out, chasing after him.

My Naughty Little Puppy

The man looked around, and his eyebrows shot up in surprise. He started to run faster, but Rascal was gaining on him.

Ellie was trailing behind them. Then she came to a stop, realizing that chasing Rascal just meant that he could chase the jogger! She set her feet firmly on the path, grabbed a handful of the extending leash, and tried to reel Rascal back in. Rascal yelped in surprise.

The jogger put on a burst of speed and disappeared out of the park, casting a grumpy look at Ellie over his shoulder.

"I'm so embarrassed!" Ellie hissed to Christy as she joined her and Bouncer.

Christy giggled. "It was definitely those shoes that caught his attention."

My Naughty Little Puppy

Rascal glared down the path as though
he thought the jogger might come back.

"Look at it this way," Christy told Ellie.
"You *were* running really fast!"

Ellie sighed and stared out across the
park. Just then, she spotted a boy whose
dog was almost as big as he was. "Oh,
look, Rascal, it's Jack and Hugo!" She
waved, and the boy waved back. Ellie
turned to Christy. "That's Jack, our friend
from puppy training. He's the one with the
Great Dane over by the swings."

Christy's mouth dropped open. "But that
dog is *huge*! He can't still be a puppy!"

"Hi, Jack!" Ellie called as Jack and
Hugo loped over to them. "This is my best
friend, Christy, and her dog, Bouncer."

Hugo and Rascal sniffed each other in a friendly way, and Bouncer eyed Hugo carefully. Bouncer probably wasn't used to being the smaller dog, Ellie thought, but then, anything was small compared to Hugo.

"Hi, Christy." Jack smiled, then looked at the boot in the girls' pile of stuff. "Why do you only have one boot?" he asked. "Has Rascal been eating shoes again?"

My Naughty Little Puppy

Ellie laughed. "No, we came to the park to practice for our school Field Day," she explained. "One of the events is a boot toss." She didn't add that the boot toss was the one competition she thought she might have a chance to do well in. She didn't find it easy to get the boot in the right place, but hopefully no one else will have practiced as much as she was going to.

"But Rascal is still crazy about shoes," she added. "Look." She showed him the boot, which was chewed all around the top. "Mom says it still keeps the water out, so there's no way she's getting me new ones."

"You're very motivated, doing extra practice," Jack said, and Ellie turned pink.

"Christy's really good at sports, but I'm

not," she explained quickly. "I run a lot faster when I'm chasing after Rascal, though."

Jack grinned. "Cool. You've got a secret weapon. Can I join in? I think our Field Day's later in the year, but it would be good to get ready."

Christy nodded. "Sure. We're going to do a running race, a skipping race, and a sack race, too." She pulled a black garbage bag out of her backpack. "I wanted to bring a pillowcase, but Mom said no, so this is the closest thing I could find to a sack."

Ellie took out a jump rope from her bag. "We can use this to make the circle to throw the boot in," she explained.

Jack grinned. "You should have brought the other boot, to give Rascal something to chew on while he's watching."

"Let's start with running," Christy suggested. "How about from here to that lamppost? That's about a hundred yards." Christy gave Ellie a stern look. "Stop looking so worried! Just pretend you're out walking with Rascal and he sees a squirrel!"

"Okay." Ellie nodded, and the three of them lined up. The dogs looked around excitedly, wondering what was going on.

"Ready, set, go!" Christy yelled, and she shot off really fast, Bouncer galloping beside her.

"Come on, Rascal!" Ellie called, and Rascal gave a sharp yap and scampered after Bouncer. Hugo launched himself

My Naughty Little Puppy

across the grass, and with his long legs
he soon overtook Rascal, who went into
a frenzy of barking. Then Hugo passed
Bouncer, too.

My Naughty Little Puppy

Ellie reached the lamppost last, and sighed.

"You weren't last by much at all!" Christy said encouragingly as the three of them sat down on the grass. "I wouldn't have thought such a huge dog could run so fast, Jack. Hugo's amazing!"

Jack patted Hugo proudly as the big dog lay down next to him, panting. "He is, isn't he?"

"But you should have seen Ellie running with Rascal earlier. . . ." said Christy to Jack, giving Ellie a wink.

Chapter Four

Rascal the Magazine Muncher

"Can we practice throwing the boot now?" Ellie said, getting to her feet. Jack had finally stopped laughing at Christy's story of Rascal and the jogger with the bright yellow sneakers.

Rascal looked interested as she picked up the boot. "It isn't for you!" Ellie told him sternly, and he flattened his ears. "Oh, it's okay, I'm not angry. But you can't chew it anymore or you'll ruin it."

My Naughty Little Puppy

She laid the jump rope out in a circle
and paced back carefully. They'd been
practicing this at school, so she knew how
far away from it she should be.

"Let me take Rascal's leash while you
throw," Christy offered. "I'll take him over
here away from the boot—he's definitely
eyeing it."

Ellie looked at the target and started
to swing the boot. She shut her eyes for a
second, and then opened them and let go.

The boot didn't hit the jump rope target,
but that was because the target wasn't there
anymore. Neither were Christy and Rascal.
They were halfway across the park, with the
jump rope trailing out of Rascal's mouth and
wrapped around his paws.

"Sorry!" Christy called back. "He surprised me. I thought he was going for the boot!"

Ellie sighed and looked at Jack, who was leaning against Hugo and practically crying with laughter.

"At least puppy training starts again on Monday," he said. "I think Rascal needs it."

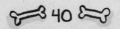

My Naughty Little Puppy

Ellie was looking forward to puppy training.
She and Rascal had already done the
beginner's class, which was where they'd
met Jack and Hugo, and now they were all
signed up for the next set of lessons, where
they would do more complicated things.

"Honestly, Rascal. I think Jack's right,"
Ellie told him, shaking her head as they
walked around the corner to her house
after saying good-bye to Christy. "What
are you doing? Dogs aren't supposed to
chase jump ropes!"

Ellie put out some food for Rascal when
she got home, and then went upstairs. She
flopped onto her bed and admired the
model stadium that was sitting on her desk.
She and Christy had been working on it

almost every afternoon after school, and it was very detailed. They'd used up three boxes of toothpicks making the metal struts around the outside of the building. Now all Ellie had to do was spray-paint it silver—Mom was going to get some silver paint on Monday—and then glue on models of athletes inside the arena. She'd already made those, but they had to wait until the silver paint was dry. Christy was cutting out hundreds of tiny pictures of people from catalogs and magazines, so that they could glue them in as the audience. It was going to be amazing when it was finished!

My Naughty Little Puppy

"Ellieeee! Look what Rascal did this time!" Max was yelling from downstairs. Ellie groaned and rushed out onto the landing. He'd only been alone for a few minutes. . . .

Max stomped up the stairs. He had Rascal under one arm and a magazine in his hand.

"What's the matter?" Ellie asked.

"I just bought it this morning!" Max scowled. "My new sports magazine! I wanted to get some practice tips out of it for Field Day. Look at it now!" He shook it open. The magazine had been chewed to pieces.

"Oh, Rascal!" Ellie said with a sigh.

Rascal stretched out and gave the magazine an interested sniff. Max snatched it back out of his reach right away. "All I did was put it down on the sofa!" he said angrily.

"I'll ask Mom if I can go down to the store and buy you a new one," Ellie promised.

"Thanks," Max muttered grumpily. He thrust Rascal into her arms and disappeared into his room.

Ellie eyed Rascal sternly. "Don't give me that proud look. I have to buy Max another magazine now, out of my allowance money, which means no more special marrowbone treats for you this week!"

Chapter Five

The Painted Puppy

Ellie was really pleased to see Jo, their puppy-training instructor, again on Monday night. Jo had given her a lot of useful tips for taking care of Rascal. She smiled to herself as she walked into the class with Dad and Rascal, wondering if Jo could teach her how to stop Rascal from stealing jump ropes and chewing magazines. . . .

Jo nodded hello as all the owners and puppies formed a circle. Jack and Hugo were there, and a couple of other people from the beginner classes. Unfortunately, Amelia and Goldie were back, too. Amelia was in sixth grade at Chase Hill, Ellie's school, and she was totally mean. She never missed a chance to make a snide comment about Rascal or Hugo. When she saw Ellie and her dad walking in, she actually groaned. Ellie blushed, but ignored her.

Jo explained that they were going to teach their dogs to come back when they were called, so that it was safe for them to be let off their leashes.

"That means we'll be able to teach the puppies to fetch, too," she pointed out. "It's great exercise for your dogs, and tons of fun."

My Naughty Little Puppy

Ellie smiled when she heard that. Rascal had been so good at fetching the Frisbee in the yard. But she hadn't yet dared to let him off the leash anywhere else. She was never quite sure if he would come back. So it sounded like these classes were going to be just what he needed.

They played a game of fetch at the end of the class. Jo had brought along some soft beanbags, which wouldn't go bouncing off all around the hall like balls would.

"Remember, we want the puppies to give the beanbags back to you, with no pulling or growling," Jo said as she handed them out. "They might find that a little tricky at first, so don't worry if they don't get it right away."

My Naughty Little Puppy

Ellie frowned, remembering Rascal
with Max's Frisbee. But maybe it would be
okay. She threw the beanbag and called,
"Rascal, fetch!" He raced off instantly,
whisking the beanbag from the floor.

Smiling to herself, Ellie reached for the
beanbag as Rascal dashed back to her.
"Drop it, Rascal!" But Rascal shook the
beanbag, wagging his tail happily. Why
on earth would he want to give up such a
fun toy? Ellie tugged it gently—and Rascal
tugged back.

My Naughty Little Puppy

Suddenly, the beanbag split down the seam, sending beans cascading all over the floor. Rascal stood in the middle of the mess and gave Ellie a look—as if to say it was all her fault!

Granddad was at Ellie's house when she, Dad, and Rascal got back.

"How was your class, Ellie?" he asked, giving her a hug.

"It was great. We're teaching the puppies how to fetch," Ellie explained. "Rascal's really good at it, except the part where he's supposed to give what he's fetched back to me. Oh, thanks, Mom," she said as Mom poured her a glass of milk. Puppy training had made her thirsty. She told Granddad all about the beanbag disaster. "But Jo said it didn't matter—they were really old beanbags."

Granddad laughed. "And your mom says you've been working on a special project for school. May I see it?"

Ellie nodded eagerly. "You'll have to come upstairs. Christy came over right after school, and we spray-painted it. It's still sticky, though."

Mom looked up. "Oh, Ellie, I opened your bedroom door and your window— the smell of that paint was very strong. I wanted to air out the room before you go to bed. Leave your door open when you come back down, please."

My Naughty Little Puppy

Ellie nodded and led Granddad upstairs to show off her model. "Ugh, you can smell the paint all the way from here," she murmured, wrinkling her nose. "Look, it's on my desk," she said proudly, pushing her door wide open.

Granddad caught his breath, and Ellie looked over at her desk, expecting him to comment on the amazing model.

Then she gasped. Their beautiful stadium was lying squashed on her desk, and there was a small, silvery-patched dog sitting in the middle of it.

My Naughty Little Puppy

"Rascal's going to be silver forever!" Ellie wailed. She was sitting on the kitchen floor, holding Rascal while Mom and Granddad tried to wipe the paint off of him.

Dad rushed into the kitchen, waving a bottle. "The vet's advice line said it wouldn't be poisonous, and to try washing it out with mild baby shampoo."

"We'll get it off, Ellie," Granddad said as Mom started to fill the kitchen sink with water. "It's only in patches, not all over him."

Ellie nodded, but tears were still trickling out of the corners of her eyes as she lifted Rascal into the sink.

My Naughty Little Puppy

"Oh, Rascal, hold still!" Mom cried as he sent a surge of water all over the floor. "We're trying to help, you silly dog!"

"It's coming off, I think," Ellie said doubtfully, peering at the sticky silvery patches, and Mom nodded.

"About time, too—this nail brush is never going to be the same again."

My Naughty Little Puppy

Ellie sighed. She still had to tell Christy their model was ruined. She lifted Rascal out of the sink and wrapped him in the old towel that Mom had given her. He snuggled against her, warm and damp, and licked her ear lovingly. "Can I go call Christy?" she gulped.

Mom glanced at the clock. "It's a little late, Ellie. She might be in bed by now." She put a wet arm around Ellie and Rascal. "Tell her at school tomorrow."

Ellie nodded and set Rascal down on the floor to dry him.

Granddad reached out and patted her shoulder. "She'll understand, love," he murmured, but Ellie could feel herself starting to cry again.

"We did so much work, and it's all
wasted! I should have put the model
somewhere safe, but I just forgot!"

"It's my fault for leaving your door
open." Mom sighed. "I didn't think, either.
All those times I've told you to be careful."

Rascal looked up at Ellie anxiously and
whined. Tears were dropping onto his nose.

"You've still got those little people you painted," Dad reminded her. "And the parts that Christy has at her house."

Ellie glanced up. "But the building part is all ruined," she sniffed. "We just don't have time to make it again. And Christy's going to be really upset."

Granddad handed Ellie a tissue. "Christy's a good friend. I know she'll be upset, but she'll come around. You're so good at making things, you and Christy will think of something."

Ellie nodded and dried her eyes. She just hoped Granddad was right.

Chapter Six

Breaking the News

Ellie yawned sleepily and rolled over, glad that it wasn't time to get up yet. Then the little ball of fur on the end of her bed wriggled and squeaked in his sleep, and Ellie woke up some more. The sun was shining through the crack in the curtains, and in the half-light she could see the silvery patch on Rascal's back that they hadn't quite been able to get out.

Ellie sat up and gazed over at her desk.

My Naughty Little Puppy

The model looked awful. How was she
ever going to tell Christy? If only she'd put
it on top of her bookshelf to dry. And if only
Mom hadn't worried so much about the
paint smell!

Ellie looked over at her clock. She
might as well get up. But maybe there
was something she could do to rescue the
model.

When Mom came in to wake Ellie
up, she found her sitting at her desk, still
trying to untangle a mess of silver-painted
toothpicks.

"Oh, dear. He really crushed it, didn't
he?"

Ellie nodded. "I'm just going to have
to start again."

My Naughty Little Puppy

"Why don't you invite Christy over tonight after school to help?" Mom said.

"I wish I didn't have to go to school," Ellie muttered. But she knew she had to.

Christy was waiting outside the school as usual, and as soon as Ellie saw her, her heart started to thud.

"What's the matter?" Christy asked when she saw Ellie's worried face.

Ellie gulped. "Rascal ruined our model!" she blurted out.

Christy stared at her. "What—the whole thing?" she whispered.

Ellie nodded miserably. "I tried to fix it this morning, but it's still a mess. I'm so sorry."

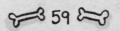

My Naughty Little Puppy

"Oh, Ellie! All that work," Christy cried.
"We spent so long on it!" She looked
up angrily. "I wish you'd teach Rascal to
behave! He really is a monster!"

Ellie felt like she was going to cry. She
didn't even try to stand up for Rascal like
she normally would. He *was* a monster!

She started to say sorry all over again,
but then the bell rang, and Christy stomped
inside the school, leaving her behind.

My Naughty Little Puppy

Ellie watched her go, her eyes filling
with tears. She'd known Christy would be
furious, but they hardly ever had fights,
and it was horrible. She had to stop crying
before anybody came to ask her what was
wrong. She dried her eyes on her sleeve
and walked slowly into class.

Christy was already at their table when
Ellie got in. Ellie glanced at her nervously as
she put away her bag, wondering whether she
should try to sit somewhere else. But Christy
looked up as she walked over to the desk.

"Sorry I yelled at you," Christy murmured.
"I know you're training Rascal, and he's not
really a monster. What happened?"

Ellie gave a little sigh of relief and sat
down. "Mom left my bedroom door open,

because of the smell of the paint. . . . Are
you really, really angry?" she added
in a whisper. Luckily, Mrs. Harley was
busy dealing with someone's forgotten
homework and hadn't caught them talking.

Christy shook her head. "No. Well, I am.
But it's like when I spilled chocolate milk shake
all over your favorite T-shirt. I didn't mean to,
and neither did you this time. I don't suppose
you've ever thought about gluing Rascal's teeth
together, have you?" She grinned.

"The silver paint almost did that. He was
covered in it. Dad had to call the vet to find
out what to do."

Christy giggled. "What are we going to
do? We only have two days till we have to
hand in the project."

"Mom says you can come over tonight so we can make something new."

Christy frowned. "Okay. But maybe you should come home with me. I'm sure mom will say yes. Then we can leave the model at my house. Bouncer doesn't really chew things." She crossed her fingers. "Well, not much, anyway . . ."

My Naughty Little Puppy

Ellie nodded. She was so glad Christy was still friends with her. "That would be great. I'll stop at home and pick up the people I made. He didn't get those. But I'd better take Rascal for a walk first. He gets even naughtier if he doesn't have any exercise."

"Why don't you bring him, too? Then he can play with Bouncer in the yard," Christy suggested. "We can ban them both from my bedroom while we're making stuff."

"Rascal would love that. Bouncer and Hugo are his best friends." Ellie gave Christy a quick hug. "Thank you for being so nice! I thought you were going to go crazy."

Christy grinned. "You owe me!"

Chapter Seven

Ellie's Brainstorm

Christy and Ellie dashed out of school when the bell rang to find their moms and ask if their plan for the evening was all right. Ellie's mom was showing Christy's mom the silver patch on Rascal's back.

"Hello, girls!" Christy's mom smiled at them both, and gave Christy a hug. "Your mom told me what happened, Ellie. Don't worry, I'm sure we can figure something out."

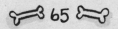

My Naughty Little Puppy

"Can we start on the new model at our house tonight, Mom?" Christy begged. "Please? Ellie can bring Rascal to play with Bouncer, then they'll both be busy and we can work on the project."

"Fine with me." Christy's mom nodded.

"Good idea," Ellie's mom said.

"I'll go home and get the people, then come over. And I'll bring the card stock," Ellie added. Then her face crumpled. "Oh, no, the card stock! We used it all up! There are only a few scraps left."

Christy bit her lip. "I didn't think of that. Is it too late to go into town and go to the art store?"

"I think it is," her mom said, looking at her watch. "Can you use something else?"

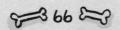

My Naughty Little Puppy

"I've got some craft stuff, but not much. We might need to make something different—not a whole stadium, I mean." Christy frowned.

Ellie nodded sadly. "It was such a cool idea. Well, I'll bring over what I've got left and we'll just have to do our best."

Ellie had Rascal's leash in one hand, and a bag of things in the other. She'd gone through her room like a whirlwind, searching for anything that she could use for their model. Hopefully when they laid it all out at Christy's, they could brainstorm something to do with it.

She was just ringing Christy's doorbell

when Rascal pulled on his leash. Christy's recycling bin was overflowing, and Rascal started sniffing around it. "No, Rascal. Leave that alone."

Rascal ignored her and tried to tug out an interesting-smelling piece of cardboard with his teeth.

"Leave it, Rascal, we don't want it!" Then Ellie smiled. Cardboard! That *was* exactly what she wanted!

When Christy opened the door, she found Ellie on her knees rooting through the bin, taking out toilet-paper tubes, cereal boxes, and even plastic milk bottles.

"What are you doing? Did Rascal knock it over?" Christy asked.

"No, but look! We can make our stadium

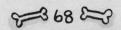

out of the recycling!" Ellie told Christy, her eyes
sparkling. Rascal picked up a toilet-paper tube
in his teeth and gave a muffled yap.

Christy sat down on the front step. "Are
you sure? It doesn't look like we could use
those pieces to make the same shape."

Ellie beamed at her. "We don't have
to. We can design our own stadium!" She
squinted her eyes as she thought. "Oh, and
we could make it really environmentally

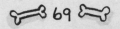

friendly, like in that project we did last fall. With a wind turbine on the roof and rainwater harvesting!"

"That does sound good." Christy smiled. "Can we build something so that when the runners are practicing, they're in a giant hamster-wheel thing, and that generates electricity for all the lights?"

"Definitely." Ellie nodded. "We can make that out of the toothpicks we had left over from the last one. Will your mom mind if we use all this? We'd better check."

Christy grabbed a handful of things from the recycling bin, and they headed into the kitchen to find Bouncer and let the two dogs out into the yard. Bouncer pricked up his ears as soon as he saw Rascal, and the pair of them ran outside together.

Christy's mom was fine with them using the recycling. In fact, she thought it was a great idea. The girls dashed upstairs, carrying all the pieces of recycling, and a big plastic sheet that she'd given them so they could lay it all out without making a mess on the bedroom carpet.

An hour later, the stadium was taking shape. It still looked like a pile of cereal boxes with towers made out of toilet-paper tubes, but Ellie could see that it was going to work. She was particularly proud of her egg carton fold-away roof—it was lucky that Christy's dad loved to make himself scrambled eggs for breakfast!

Christy looked at it with her head to one

side. "When it's sprayed silver, I think it'll
look even better than the old one. And no
one else will have a project like it."

The mention of silver paint reminded
Ellie about Rascal. "I hope the dogs are still
okay in the yard."

Christy jumped up and peered out of her
window. "Well, Bouncer's asleep under the
bench—I can see his tail sticking out. I can't
see Rascal, though."

Ellie ran over to look as well. "I can't

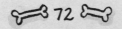

see him, either. We'd better go and check,
just in case. . . ."

The girls hurried downstairs and through
the back door. Bouncer woke up as they
came out, and thumped his tail sleepily. But
there was no sign of Rascal.

"Where can he be?" Ellie muttered,
running down the path. "Rascal! Rascal!"
She peered behind the shed, wondering if
he'd gone digging—he loved to dig holes..
But no muddy little dog poked his head
out. "He must be here somewhere. He
couldn't have escaped, could he?"

"No, there is a hole under the fence,
but it isn't big enough. . . ." Christy's eyes
widened. "Oh, no. It's not big enough for
Bouncer, but Rascal could get through it!"

My Naughty Little Puppy

She ran over to the wheelbarrow standing by the shed. "Help me push this to the fence so we can look over. Quietly!" she hissed. "Mr. Simpson next door really hates dogs— he always complains that Bouncer barks too much."

They pushed the wheelbarrow up against the fence and scrambled into it to peer over.

"Oh, no . . ." Christy gasped.

The yard on the other side of the fence was immaculate, as though every blade of grass had been measured. And snuffling around the rosebushes was a small white-and-brown (and silver) dog. Rascal looked up at them and wagged his tail happily.

"Rascal! Rascal, here!" Ellie tried to use

My Naughty Little Puppy

the firm tone of voice that Jo had talked
about at training, but it came out all high
and worried, and Rascal ignored her.

"Should I go get some treats to tempt
him with?" Christy suggested.

"Hey! What do you two think you're

My Naughty Little Puppy

doing?" A loud yell echoed across the yard as the neighbor's back door flew open and Mr. Simpson tramped down the yard path. "What's that in my roses? Get out of there, you little menace!"

As the girls quickly tried to get down, the wheelbarrow wobbled, tipping them into a muddy patch of flower bed.

Mr. Simpson stuck his head over the fence and glared down at them.

Before he could say a word, Rascal

My Naughty Little Puppy

shot through the gap under the fence
and bolted over to Ellie. He looked very
scared. As Ellie scooped him up, he buried
his head under her arm, quivering.

"That dog has just been *waltzing* through
my rosebushes!" Mr. Simpson roared.

"I'm really sorry," Christy squeaked. "We
didn't realize he could get through the gap
under the fence. He's just visiting. . . ."

"Hmph! Well, luckily this time he didn't
do any damage. I suggest you don't let him
visit again!" Mr. Simpson snapped, and
stomped away.

"Oh, Christy, he's really mean. I'm sorry
for getting you into trouble!" Ellie said.

"Don't worry," Christy replied. "Mr.
Simpson's always angry about something.

My Naughty Little Puppy

I kicked a ball over the fence last week, and when he threw it back, he'd written a message on it in marker. It said that next time he'd 'accidentally' stab it with his yard fork!"

Ellie giggled. "He's horrible!"

Christy nodded and gave Ellie a hug. "I think he likes being grumpy. He probably enjoyed having the chance yell at us!"

Chapter Eight

The Perfect Project

Ellie decided she'd better take Rascal home after that, in case he did anything else. She left the paint with Christy so she could spray their model and leave it to dry overnight. They planned to add the finishing touches after school the next day, so it would be ready to take in on Thursday morning.

"Did you manage to make something nice?" Mom asked when they arrived home. "And did Rascal behave?"

My Naughty Little Puppy

"Well . . . we made an awesome new model. But Rascal got a little bored in Christy's yard and he went . . . visiting."

"Oh, no! Not to Christy's grumpy next-door neighbor? Her mom's told me about him before."

"Yes," Ellie admitted. "But he didn't actually dig anything up!"

"That dog!" her mom muttered. "When we decided to get a Jack Russell, Ellie, nobody told me that they were known to be one of the stubbornest, hardest-to-train, generally naughty dogs there are."

"And the most adorable!" Ellie reminded her, holding Rascal up so he could nudge Mom's cheek with his damp little nose.

My Naughty Little Puppy

"Hmmm . . ." was all her mom said, but she did pet him.

"Actually, Mom, I think our new project is going to be better than the old one. The new design's really green and creative, and no one else will have anything like it," Ellie told her proudly. "Rascal did us a favor!"

Ellie was right. Mrs. Harley was very impressed by their model on Thursday when they set it up on the project table at school.

"With a wind turbine? Very inventive, girls!" She made a little note in her folder.

Ellie and Christy grinned at each other. Their project definitely looked the best.

"And look, Sinead and Lily built a model of the same stadium we were making," Ellie pointed out. "So it's good that we ended up doing something different."

Mr. Turner arrived later that morning, and Mrs. Harley showed him the projects. Everyone whispered excitedly, and Ellie and Christy both crossed their fingers.

My Naughty Little Puppy

"Well done, everyone. There were some really good ideas, but we've chosen Ellie and Christy's as the best project from this class." Mr. Turner smiled at them. "A wonderful use of recycled materials, girls. We're going to put your model on display in the entrance hall, so the parents can all see it tomorrow."

"We should say thank you to Rascal for spoiling the old one!" Christy whispered, and Ellie nodded. Rascal really *had* done them a favor!

That afternoon they had a long Field Day practice session, and Ellie felt like she must have tripped over at least a hundred hurdles.

My Naughty Little Puppy

"Can't I just pretend to be sick tomorrow?" she muttered to Christy, but her friend shook her head firmly.

"No. Because you're going to be amazing at the boot toss. You almost won when you did it just now! Why don't you ask your mom if I can come over for a while tonight, so we can practice running more without lots of people watching?"

"But people *will* be watching tomorrow!" Ellie pointed out.

Christy frowned. "Maybe you could pretend you're invisible, or something?"

"I wish I was." Ellie sighed.

Christy rolled her eyes and made a face.

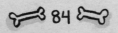

My Naughty Little Puppy

"All right," said Ellie. "I'll ask Mom if you can come over for one last practice."

"Run down to the end of the lawn, touch the lilac tree, and run back," Christy said.

"And try not to trip over your feet," Max added, poking his head around the kitchen door.

"That's mean!" Christy said.

"Yee-es," Max agreed. "But true."

"I bet I'm faster than you," Christy told Max, and he gave a disbelieving snort.

"Race you! Lilac tree and back—or are you too scared?"

Max smiled pityingly. "I'm two years older than you, and I'm a boy."

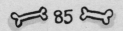

My Naughty Little Puppy

"Chicken," Christy teased.

Max shrugged. "Okay. I could do with some practice for tomorrow, too. I was just warning you."

"She's really fast," Ellie told him. "She's going to win the hundred-meter dash in our grade, for sure."

Christy grinned at her as she and Max lined up. Ellie sat down on the edge of the patio and hugged Rascal tightly, so he wouldn't try to join in. With her luck, he'd manage to trip Christy *and* Max.

"Ready, set, go!" Ellie yelled, and they shot off down the yard. They were neck and neck as they touched the lilac tree, but Max was taller and stronger, and he put on a huge burst of speed on the run back up the yard. There was no way he was going to be beaten by his younger sister's friend. But he only *just* came in first.

"Hey, you *are* good," he said admiringly.

"You . . . still . . . won!" Christy panted.

Max sat down next to Ellie. "I'm sorry. I shouldn't have teased you about Field Day. You know what you should do?"

Ellie shook her head cautiously. She wasn't sure if Max was still teasing her.

"Practice the three-legged race with Christy. If you figure out how to step together, you've got a really good chance. I'll show you, here."

He pulled Ellie to her feet, grabbed the jump rope that was lying on the patio, and tied her leg to Christy's. "You go 'middle, side, middle, side,' and don't get mixed up. That's all there is to it."

Ellie looked at him doubtfully. It couldn't be that easy, could it? "Middle," she said slowly, and she and Christy put their tied feet forward. Rascal trotted after them, looking confused.

"Say it together," Max told them.

"Middle, side, middle, side, middle, side," Ellie and Christy chanted, wobbling down the lawn, and then they laughed out loud.

It worked!

"Told you so," Max said. "Rascal wants to join in, though. Maybe it ought to be a seven-legged race!"

Chapter Nine

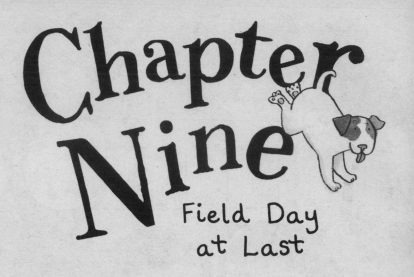

Field Day at Last

Ellie waved at Mom and Rascal as her class walked out onto the school field. There were flags hung up all along the fence, and the moms and dads were sitting on blankets, ready to watch the Field Day events. Lots of little brothers and sisters were running around, and there were quite a few dogs, too.

Ellie's mom was sitting next to Christy's mom, with Christy's little sister, Jade, but she hadn't brought Bouncer. Although Christy

had begged for him to come, her mom
had said Jade was enough to worry about
without a dog there, too. Jade was playing
with Rascal and seemed to be trying to put
her comfort blankie on him like a cloak.

"Good afternoon, everyone! Welcome
to Field Day," Mr. Turner announced over
the PA system. "So that we have time to
give everyone a chance at all the events,
we'll be moving the classes around the
field. Each class has been divided into four
groups for most of the races."

He went on to read out a list of where
all the different classes should be. Ellie's
grade was starting with the hurdles, Ellie's
worst race. At least she was in the first
group, so she could get it over with.

Please don't let me fall over, she thought to herself as Mrs. Harley waved for them to start. It hadn't seemed to matter in the practices whether she went as fast as she could or slowly and carefully—she still tripped over the hurdles.

My Naughty Little Puppy

So Ellie simply pretended she was racing across the park with Rascal, jumping over sections of long grass. It worked very well for the first four hurdles, but somehow the "long grass" got twisted around her ankles on the last one, and she tumbled over.

Ellie clambered to her feet, scarlet-cheeked. She could hear all the mothers worrying if she was hurt. She jogged to the finish line, and slunk away to hide in a group of other girls from her class.

"It's okay." Christy gave her a hug. "Remember the boot toss. You'll be really good at that."

Ellie nodded gratefully. Just the skipping and the sack race to get through first. At least *everybody* fell over in that one. . . .

My Naughty Little Puppy

Ellie lifted the red boot, and swung it gently back and forth. She grinned hopefully over at Mom and Rascal, who were standing close by, watching.

Rascal gave an excited bark and dragged on the leash to get closer to Ellie, but Mom pulled him back and got him to sit. Ellie watched proudly as Rascal sat down perfectly and lifted his nose to gobble up the treat Mom held out for him. He looked like an advertisement for puppy training!

She shook herself firmly. She had to concentrate. Max had won three races already, and Christy had won the skipping race. Ellie at least wanted to get her boot

My Naughty Little Puppy

in the center of the circle!

Ellie stepped up to the line and threw the boot. It was looking good, and like it might go in! Then a small white-and-brown blur darted in front of her and made a flying leap for the boot. It was a fantastic jump—even Ellie could see that, at the same time as she was squirming with embarrassment.

My Naughty Little Puppy

Rascal pranced over to her, tail wagging so fast it blurred, and laid the boot lovingly at her feet. It was the first time he'd ever given her anything he'd fetched, Ellie realized. She crouched down and gave him a pat as she took the boot.

Mom raced over and grabbed Rascal's leash. "Oh, Ellie, I'm sorry. He was sitting so nicely. . . . I didn't notice he was about to chase the boot."

"Would you like another try?" Mrs. Harley asked as Ellie handed her the boot, but Ellie shook her head. All she wanted was to go and hide behind a tree at the far end of the field.

My Naughty Little Puppy

All of Ellie's classmates were jumping up and down and cheering. It was the final of the hundred-meter dash for their grade, and the competition was stiff. Ellie stood with her mom and Christy's mom, cheering Christy on.

"Look at that boy—he's so tall!" Christy's mom murmured as Christy and the others lined up. "She can't possibly run faster than him."

But she could. Christy sped down the track, beating the boy just by a hair. She danced over to them, beaming.

"Great job!" Ellie cried. "I told you you'd win."

Christy's mom gave her a hug. "That was amazing! I'm so proud of you!"

Ellie saw her mom behind them, smiling,

My Naughty Little Puppy

and wished she had won something. *I trained Rascal to fetch!* she told herself firmly. *That's really great. And useful.*

"Mom, where's Jade?" Christy asked suddenly, and Christy's mom whirled around.

"She's sitting on the blanket, isn't she?"

But apart from Jade's little pink blankie lying there in a heap, the blanket was bare.

Chapter Ten

Rascal the Hero

Christy's mom shook her head. "Jade was there a second ago," she said. "She was sitting there with her blankie. She couldn't have just disappeared. . . ."

But she had. Christy's mom decided to stay by the blanket in case Jade came back, while Ellie's mom went to get Mr. Turner to make an announcement over the PA system. Meanwhile, Christy and Ellie set off across the field to search for Jade.

My Naughty Little Puppy

Jade wasn't sitting with any of the other children scattered around the field, and she wasn't in the crowd watching the races.

"What about the food stall?" Christy suggested, and she and Ellie tore across the field to check. But she wasn't there.

"Where else can we look?" Christy said, sounding panicky. She sometimes complained about how annoying Jade was, but she really adored her. It was like Ellie whining about Max and Lila.

"We have a missing child. Everyone please look out for Jade Lassiter, age three. She must be somewhere on the field. . . ." announced Mr. Turner over the PA system.

Ellie swallowed. The announcement made it feel even more serious.

My Naughty Little Puppy

The races stopped, and people started searching all over the field. Where else was there to look?

"I know!" Ellie suddenly remembered a TV show she'd watched about police dogs. She grabbed Christy's hand and dragged her back to their blanket.

"Jade's not here!" Christy protested. "What are you doing?"

"Getting this," Ellie answered, snatching up Jade's blankie. "Now we need Rascal."

Ellie's mom was comforting Christy's mom. "What do you want him for?" she asked as Ellie tried to take Rascal's leash. "Ellie, this isn't the time . . ."

"Rascal can find her!" Ellie explained. "Look, Rascal." She held the pink blankie

under his nose. "Jade carries this around
everywhere, doesn't she? It'll smell like
her," Ellie went on. "Rascal, where's Jade?
Find Jade, Rascal."

Rascal sniffed at it with interest and
looked up at Ellie, his eyes sparkling. He'd
been bored, sitting around all afternoon
when there was a field he could have
been running all over. Now Ellie was
playing a good game.

My Naughty Little Puppy

He set off, looking this way and that, ears pricked and tail wagging. Ellie followed him, pulling Christy by the hand. "Good boy, Rascal. Keep going."

Rascal trotted across the field and around the corner of the school building.

"He can't be right, Ellie—there's nothing here," Christy murmured.

"He is leading us *somewhere*," Ellie told her. But even she was beginning to doubt Rascal, just a little bit.

Then Rascal stopped in front of the little metal shed where the sports equipment was kept. He looked up at Ellie, his tail wagging frantically.

"She's in there?" Ellie asked him, and Rascal pulled against his leash, dragging

My Naughty Little Puppy

her over to the door. Then he looked up
again and barked loudly, almost as if he
was saying, "There! Told you so!"

As Ellie opened the door, Rascal raced
inside. At the back of the little shed, curled
up on a pile of old gym mats, was Jade,
holding on to the corner of a sack-race
sack instead of her beloved pink blankie.

"Hello, Rascal!" she said sleepily.

My Naughty Little Puppy

"You found her!" Christy squealed. "Rascal, you smart, wonderful dog!"

Christy ran off at top speed, and soon her mom and Ellie's mom and half the school were all gathered around the shed.

"Ah, isn't she sweet?"

"And that little dog found her?"

"You should be very proud of Rascal, Ellie," Mrs. Harley told her.

Christy's mom handed Ellie some money. "Once you finish your last race, go and buy Rascal a reward from the food stall. They had some nice ham sandwiches earlier."

Ellie picked Rascal up. As she walked back to the field, lots of people reached out to pet him, like he was a hero. She felt so proud, she couldn't stop smiling.

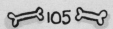

My Naughty Little Puppy

"Are you ready?" Christy asked seriously. "Ellie, stop laughing! Remember, Max said we had to concentrate."

Ellie nodded, but she still had a silly smile on her face. She wasn't sure she could concentrate on the three-legged race. She didn't mind if she lost all the events now. Rascal was a hero, and he was hers!

"GO!"

"Middle, side, middle, side!" she and Christy muttered, and they stomped their way down the course, staying in rhythm.

Ellie risked a quick glance over her shoulder. They were winning! Max was

My Naughty Little Puppy

running alongside them, with Rascal safely on the leash. "Come on, Ellie, come on, Christy! You're almost there!" he shouted.

But Jessie and Lydia were gaining on them. "Faster!" Christy hissed. "Middle, side, middle, side! Yes!"

They'd done it! She and Christy had actually won the three-legged race!

They collapsed in a giggling heap
by the finish line. Max dashed over and
gave Ellie a lightning-fast hug, in case any
of his friends noticed. "You did it!"

Mrs. Harley laughed. "Well done, girls!
That was the last race. Time to give out the
prizes now."

"Excellent!" Christy grinned.

"Greedy! You already won two races!"
Ellie laughed. They stood listening to
Mr. Turner as he read out his long list of
winners. All the way through kindergarten,
first grade, second grade . . .

"And in fourth grade we have a special
mention for Ellie Thomas, and an honorary
member of the class—her dog, Rascal.
Great job, Rascal, for finding little Jade,

who was lost earlier. Let's give a round of applause for Rascal, everyone!"

Ellie's mom held him up, and Rascal barked with excitement.

"And I'm delighted to say that Ellie, along with Jade's big sister, Christy, have won the three-legged race. Great job, Ellie and Christy!"

As the announcements went on, Ellie cheered for Christy winning all those races, and for Max winning practically everything in sight. She didn't mind at all. She had Rascal, and he was a rescue dog.

"Come on, let's go and buy him a sandwich!" Christy suggested.

The moms running the food stall had heard all about Rascal, and insisted that

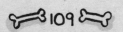

My Naughty Little Puppy

Ellie needed some cupcakes for thinking so quickly, and that Christy should take some to cheer up Jade, too.

The girls raced back with their piled-up plates.

"Here you are, boy." Ellie tore the ham sandwich up into little pieces and placed them on the paper plate. Rascal gulped them down delightedly, and then looked around, hoping for more.

"We should make him a medal," Christy's mom said.

Ellie laughed. "I think he'd rather just have another sandwich." And she picked him up, whispering, "I'll make you one at home. You're a star, Rascal!"

WOOF
magazine

Don't miss

Rascal's naughtiness is annoying everyone, so Mom and Dad decide it's time to take him to dog-training classes. Ellie thinks this is a great plan. But wherever Rascal goes, trouble is never far behind. . . .

Q: My dog won't stop chewing our furniture and belongings. Help!
—Annoyed Dog Owner

A: Your dog may be chewing things he shouldn't because he's bored, wants attention, or misses you when you're out. Try these tips:

• Don't leave your belongings out where he can get to them, and use anti-chewing furniture sprays to keep him away.
• Give him plenty of attention and exercise—he won't be so much trouble if he's too tired to chew!
• Ask at your pet store for toys and chews that are safe to leave with him. Don't give him old shoes because he'll confuse them with new ones!
• If you catch your dog chewing the wrong thing, interrupt him with a loud noise, or shout, "No!" Remove the object, saying, "Give." Offer him a chew toy instead, praising him for taking it. Never shout at him *after* he's misbehaved, since he won't understand what he's being scolded for!